I0669651

Phil May

Phil May's sketch-book

Fifty cartoons

Phil May

Phil May's sketch-book
Fifty cartoons

ISBN/EAN: 9783741191626

Manufactured in Europe, USA, Canada, Australia, Japa

Cover: Foto ©Andreas Hilbeck / pixelio.de

Manufactured and distributed by brebook publishing software
(www.brebook.com)

Phil May

Phil May's sketch-book

PHIL MAY'S

SKETCH-BOOK

FIFTY CARTOONS

POPULAR EDITION

LONDON
CHATTO & WINDUS, 111 ST MARTIN'S LANE
1897

MR. PHIL MAY ON HIMSELF.[1]

I NEVER had a drawing lesson in my life, but I can't remember a time when I didn't draw. At the time of the Franco-German War, when I was a child of three or four, I used to draw imaginary pictures of the battles—bristling bayonets, cannonade, and smoke—more particularly smoke. Later I drew portraits of the actors and actresses who played at Leeds, where I lived. When I was sixteen I made up my mind to come to London, and see whether I couldn't make a living with my pencil. So I took a ticket, third-class single, and tried my fortune. It was a hard fight. I had no friends and no introductions worth speaking of. There were comparatively few illustrated papers in those days, and prices ranged very low. I had a good many bad quarters of an hour. Once, I remember, I was in such a desperate mood that I seriously contemplated burgling a coffee-stall—fortunately there was a policeman near, so I did not. But in six months I was beginning to get on. I worked for 'Society,' the 'Penny Illustrated Paper,' the 'St. Stephen's Review,' and the 'Pictorial World.' In November 1885 I went to Australia to join the staff of the 'Sydney Bulletin,' stayed there three years, and afterwards lived in Paris, until I began my work for the 'Daily Graphic.' 'Parson and Painter,' which helped my reputation a good deal, appeared in 'St. Stephen's.' It had no effect whatever on the circulation of the paper, and I had no idea that it was going to attract any attention; but when the series was published in volume form 30,000 copies were very quickly sold.

If a man really has any originality in him it is bound to find its way out. No doubt the art schools turn out plenty of men who can do excellent studies, but they are absolutely incapable of composing good pictures. That is the fault of the men, not of the schools. On the other hand, the man who undergoes no formal training endures many disadvantages. If he loses nothing else, he loses time. There are so many things that don't come by intuition, but have to be found out. You can find them out in two ways—by being told, or by trying and failing, and then trying again. I have found out a good many things in this latter way, and

[1] From *The Sketch*, March 22, 1893.

I don't recommend it; it is very roundabout. Besides, perspective and anatomy are dull studies, and there is always the temptation not to bother about them beyond a certain point.

Many people have the idea that my work is, as they say, 'dashed off.' They think that because, when it is finished, there are so few lines in it. But they are wrong. What reputation I have made I ascribe to very careful preparation of my sketches. First of all, I get the rough idea of the picture. Sometimes it is suggested by a story I have heard, or by something I have seen. Sometimes it occurs to me spontaneously. I sketch a rough outline of the picture I want to draw, and from the general idea of this rough outline I never depart. Then I make several studies from the model in the poses which the picture requires, and re-draw my figures from these studies. The next step is to draw the picture completely, carefully putting in every line necessary to fulness of detail; and the last, to select the particular lines that are essential to the effect I want to produce, and take all the others out. That is how it is done.

My types are all individuals. I am constantly on the look-out for the individual who embodies a type. When I am drawing a picture with several figures in it I often go out into the street to look for types. But I am collecting them at all times and in all places, more particularly in trains and omnibuses. I collected fifty or so in a recent visit to Battle, and a lot more, of a different sort, when I was on the Riviera last spring. They will all come in useful some day. Australia has supplied me with any number. A quaint old Sydney clergyman whom I know figured very usefully not so long ago in an allegorical and 'up-to-date' presentment of 'The Temptation of St. Anthony,' and a well-known Australian curate was the original of the parson in 'Parson and Painter.' I am told that when the book came to be circulated in Greater Britain this gentleman's sermons acquired a sudden and enormous popularity, with the result that he unexpectedly found himself addressing his exhortations to many persons who had previously been far too negligent of their religious privileges.

CONTENTS.

CONTENTS.

"I'm glad they've got a fine day for their procession, but it's
a thing as I don't take much interest in myself."

VISITOR. 'Some of your ancestors, I suppose?'

PARVENU. 'Bless you! I ain't got no ancestors. My ancestors is all dead.'

JONES (*to Brown, who has been to a ball at Robinson's*). ' Many women there ?'
BROWN. ' No; only their mothers.'

DISTINGUISHED AMATEUR (*who has been cast for the part of Sir Toby Belch*). ' I suppose I shall want a little padding ?'

COSTUMIER. 'Certainly;' (*shouting*) 'Ernest, bring down a full-size stomach.'

'For I am a Man of the Town.'

FAT OLD PARTY (*who for the last hour has been eating without stopping*). 'Excuse me, Miss, but my eyesight is very bad; would you mind telling me if I've eaten everything on the *menu*?'

FAME.

He. 'When I was in America I met the famous Mr. Edison. Of course, you've heard of him?'
She. 'Oh, yes! He invented the Edison Lighthouse, didn't he?'

OLD SAILOR. "Yes, I've 'ad nearly every bone in my body broke at different times—arm broke, leg broke, nose broke, thigh broke—"

POTMAN. "Ave ye ever bin stone-broke?"

'That was an awfully funny joke you made last night. I wish I could say it was mine!'
'You will, my boy; you will!'

'Deuced funny!'

PAT (shouting after Tommy Atkins). 'Who shtole the cat!'
TOMMY. ''Oo stole yer bloomin' country?'

'So kind and thoughtful of you to send me this little puppy. So *like* you!'

'Oh! please, Missus says, will you make the knives extra sharp, 'cause we've got a chicken for
dinner, and Master can't eat it if it's tough.'

XVIII

GERMAN PROFESSOR. 'How beautiful everything is in Nature!'

MEAN!

Conversation overheard at a Railway Station. "Yes, Bill 'ad a quid as a present, and a quid to
git married with, and 'e never paid me that seven and a tanner 'e owes me!"

YOUNG LADY. 'Shepherd, I am told that you can tell the difference between every individual sheep. How do you do it?'

SHEPHERD. 'Well, Miss, much in the same way as I could tell yer pretty face in a million!'

(He gets sixpence for the secret.)

CATCH THIS BIRD WITH CHAFF!

LANDLORD. 'Now, John, you must join the Association formed to benefit Landlords, Tenants, and Labourers. We shall soon revert to the good old times.'

JOHN. 'Yes, sir; 'igh rents for landlords and low wages for men. Some'ows, I don't see my way to join.'

'I suppose you've travelled a good deal in your time?'

'Oh, yes; I've been to Scarborough and Margate, and I remember quite well a-goin' to London when I was a lad. I went to the Zoological Gardens, and saw the lions and unicorns and them sort of animals.'

Scene : Corridor of first-class Hotel.
Time : Seven a.m.

Mr. Briggs (*just come from Yorkshire to give important evidence in a late case, and staying at an hotel for the first time*). 'Where's t' kitchen ?'
Astonished Chambermaid. 'What do you want the kitchen for ?'
Mr. Briggs. 'I want to wash mesen.'

XXV

XXVI

"Give us a bite of yer apple, Billy!"

"Sha'n't!"

"Well, leave us a bit of the core!"

"There ain't goin' to be no core!"

XXVII

SWEETHEART (*back from the wars*). "Gracious! how she's grown!"

Tourist. 'Fine head that child's got. He'll be a Gladstone.'
Fond Mother. 'Drat the man! that can't be: his father's a Conservative.'

PATERFAMILIAS — 'What do you expect to be if you grow up such a dunce?'
YOUNG HOPEFUL — 'A masher.'

GENEROUS

' Give yer a orange!   Wot for?'

' 'Cos that one I bought last week was a bad un.'

' Where is it ?'

' I gave it to my sister.'

'Have you ever been photographed, uncle?'
'Yes, Tommy.'
'What for?'

"Oh, uncle! when I grow up, shall I have a face like yours if I'm wicked?"

ONE OF OUR ALIENS.

' Do you vant to buy a thuit of clothes as vos made for the Prinsh of Vales ?'

XXXV

'Do you want a model, sir?'
'No! Go away! I'm busy.'
'Well, lend me sixpence.'
'Certainly not; I don't know you.'
'Garn! Lend me sixpence, and I'll give you twopence to get your 'air cut.'

Tell me 'ow u du it'.

AT APPY 'AMPSTEAD ON EASTER MONDAY.

'I don't care for them 'ats, 'Arriet; everybody's a-wearin' of 'em!'

XL

AT THE ALHAMBRA.

'Waiter, bring me a brandy-and-soda.'

'Beg pardon, miss, but we're not allowed to serve ladies.'

'I'm not a lady!'

'Wot sort of a stone do yer call that as yer've got in yer ring, 'Arriet?'
'Well? dunno; but my chap says as 'e thinks as it's a 'Ammersmith.'

BILL'S NOT IN IT WHEN JACK'S ASHORE.

A VISION

THE IRONY OF CIRCUMSTANCE.

A FEW PARTING WORDS OF ADVICE.

FATHER *(to son who is just going out into the world).* And remember one thing: Never you marry a gal as is richer than you. When I married your mother I 'ad thirty bob and she 'ad two pun' ten—and she's never ceased to throw it in my face ever since.'

'With a neck like that, what a fine thing it must be to be thirsty!'

A VACATION EXERCISE.

SIR HENRY IRVING.

FRED HALL

L

J. WATTS

CAPTAIN MACHELL.

THE DUKE OF WESTMINSTER

LORD ALINGTON.

COLONEL NORTH.

SOME SPORTING CELEBRITIES.